A BED OF YOUR OWN!

by Mij Kelly

and Mary McQuillan

First edition for the United States and Canada in 2011 by
Barron's Educational Series, Inc.

First published in 2011 by Hodder Children's Books, 338 Euston Road,
London NW1 3BH Great Britain

All inquiries should be addressed to:
Barron's Educational Series, Inc.
250 Wireless Boulevard, Hauppauge, New York 11788
www.barronseduc.com

ISBN: 978-0-7641-4768-5

Library of Congress Control No. 2011921277

Product conforms to all applicable CPSC and CPSIA 2008 standards.
No lead or phthalate hazard.

Manufactured in China
Manufactured by Toppan Leefung Printing Ltd. China
Date of Manufacture: May 2011

9 8 7 6 5 4 3 2 1

To Cerys and Dylan – MK

To Finn with love – MMcQ

A BED OF YOUR OWN!

Mij
Kelly

Mary
McQuillan

BARRON'S

This is the story of Suzy Sue,
ready for bed, just like you.

She **brushed** her teeth.
She picked up her Ted...

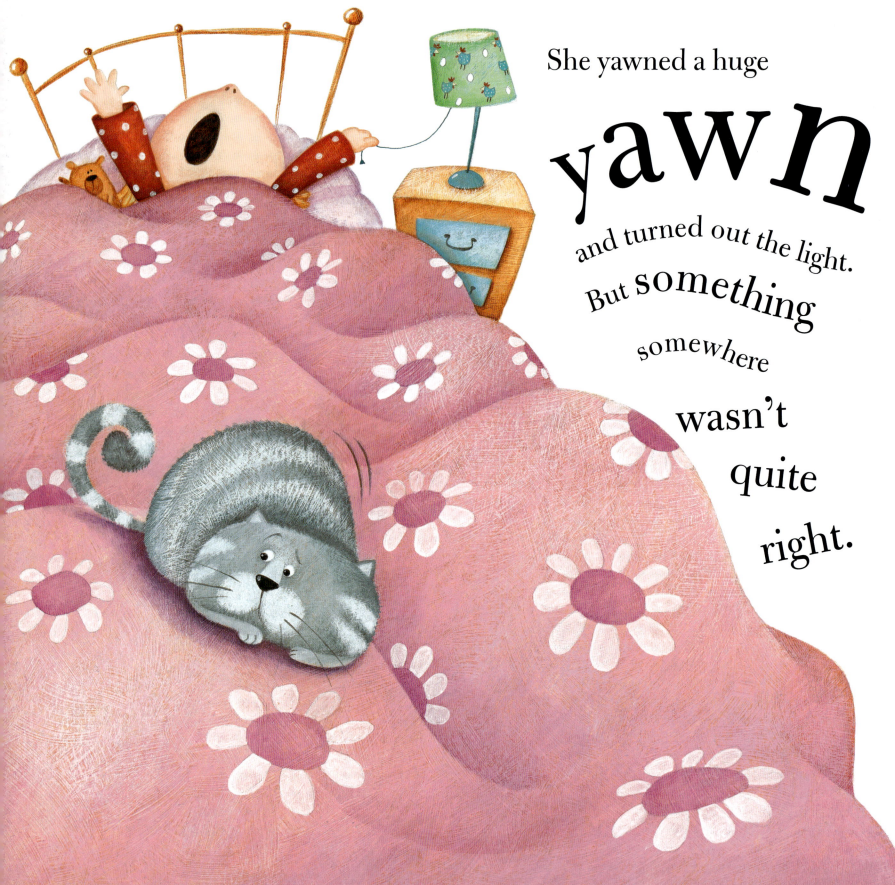

She clambered and climbed into her bed.

She yawned a huge

yawn

and turned out the light. But **something** somewhere wasn't quite right.

"I'm **squished**. I'm **squashed**.
I'm **uncomfy!**" she said.

"I think there's something wrong with the bed."

"I know!" said the cow.
"This bed's **far too small**.
I've tried and I've tried,
but I **can't sleep** at all."

Oh, what a **shock!**
What a **drama**
of **dramas!**

A **COW** in the bed – a cow in pajamas!

"What are you doing?" said Suzy Sue.

"What do you think?"
said the cow, with a **moO.**
"I'm **trying** to go
to sleep, of course."

"Oh, please do be quiet!"
grumbled the horse.

"How in the world can I get a nap

with the pair of you going

yappity-yap?"

Oh, what a **shock!** What a **bolt** from the blue!

A **horse** in the bed, with his cuddly toys, too!

And when Suzy Sue fell back in a heap, what she thought was a pillow...

... was really a **sheep.**

"How can I sleep? How can I doze?

Please, please, please,

leb go ob by nose!"

Oh, what a **shock**!

What a **dreadful** surprise!

But by now Suzy Sue was getting quite wise.

She threw back the covers. She called,

loud and clear,

"Are **any more** animals hiding in here?"

"Just little me,"
somebody said...

... and Suzy Sue

fell out

of the bed.

Goodness gracious!

Oh, golly! Oh, gosh!

No wonder the bed was a **terrible squash.**
No wonder **nobody** could get any sleep,

with a **goat** and a **horse** and a **COW** and a **sheep**

all tossing and turning,
all hogging the covers
and fighting for pillows and kicking
each other –

"For goodness sake!" yawned Suzy Sue.

"What on earth's got into you?

Don't you have a bed of your OWN?"

"We can't sleep there,"
said the sheep
with a groan.

"It's too hot!" "It's too cold!"
"It's too dark!" "It's too light!"
"There's something about it that isn't quite right!"

But Suzy Sue was stern and strong.
She led them back where they belonged.

She tucked them up, and then she read
a book about going to bed.

She hugged them all and said,

"Good night."

But just as she went to turn out the light...

... she had an idea, and suddenly said, "It's all very well this going to bed, but what really matters is **falling asleep.**"

"But that's the **hardest** part!" said the sheep.

So Suzy Sue climbed in the bed.
"What you have to do," she said,
"is feel how your bed is all **comfy** and **cozy**...

...Feel how it makes you all d r o w s y and d o z y.
Feel a safe, soothing softness beginning to spread
from the tips of your toes to the
top of your head.

And all of your worries
are wafting away,
like a bunch of
balloons on a cloudless
spring day,

and you're in a boat, floating downstream,
drifting away on a beautiful dream."

In the silence that followed, you could hear a pin drop.

"Go on," said the cow, "Please don't stop."

"Oh, dear," said the goat. "Oh, dear. Oh, dear.
She's fallen asleep. But she can't sleep here!"

"She's **hogging** the bed."

"She's starting to **snore.**"

"She'll keep us **awake.** It's happened before."

zZZZZZZ

"Oh silly Suzy Sue," they said.
"Come on, let's take you back to bed.
See, each of us has our own place to rest.

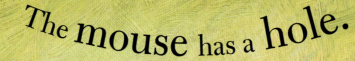

The mouse has a hole.

The hen has a nest.

The **pig** has a **sty**
(it's smelly but snug).

The **dog** has his **house**.

The **cat**
has her **rug**.

They ALL have beds,

and you do too.

So snuggle down, Suzy Sue."

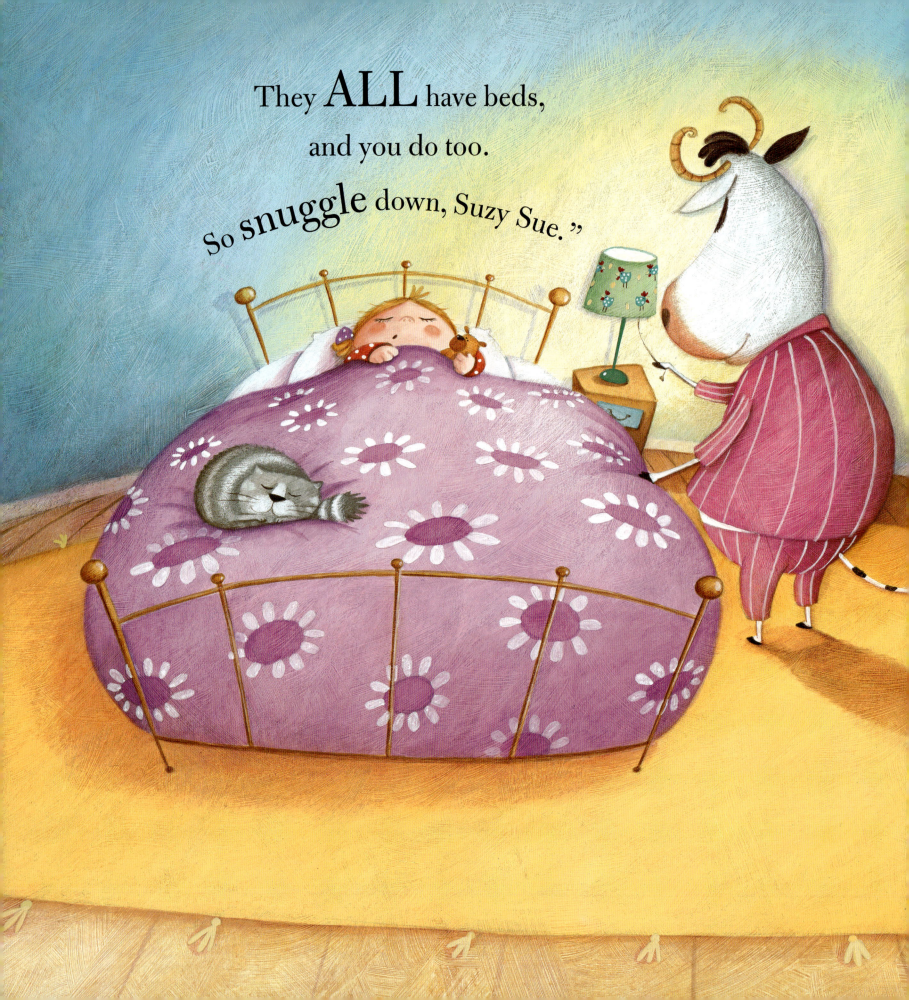

That was the story of Suzy Sue,
safe in her own bed,

– like you should be, too!